Shelly the Turtle

By Jeannie Hayes

Illustrated by Angie Scordato

Shelly the Turtle lived by Mr. Brown's farm.
Every morning, Sammy the Rooster would wake her up.

"Cock-A-Doodle-Doo!" crowed Sammy.

"Oh my," sighed Shelly,
 from inside her warm shell.
"Time to wake up."
 Shelly stretched her neck
 and brought her head out of her shell.
 Then she stretched her legs.

"Pop! Pop! Pop! Pop!"
Each leg popped out of the
shell. Shelly plodded over
to the farm. "I wonder what all
of the animals are up to today!"

Shelly walked over to Harold the Horse. "Hello Harold," said Shelly. "What are you doing?"

"I'm practicing for a race," said Harold. "Look how fast I can run!"

Clippity clop! Clippity clop! Harold ran all the way around the field. He was so fast!

"I wish I could run like that," said Shelly. "Turtles are too slow."
"There must be something else you're good at," said Harold.
He went back to running in circles. **Clippity clop! Clippity clop!**

Shelly kept walking to see what other animals were out to play. She found Pearl the Pig. "**Oink!** Hi Shelly!" said Pearl. "I'm playing in the mud!"

Pearl lay down and rolled over and over. With every roll, her pink skin got messier and messier.

"**Oink! Oink!** Playing in the mud is so much fun! I love to get dirty!"squealed Pearl.

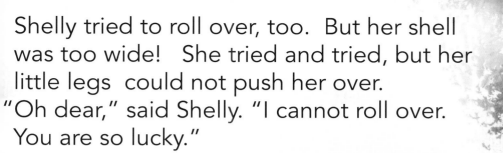

Shelly tried to roll over, too. But her shell was too wide! She tried and tried, but her little legs could not push her over.
"Oh dear," said Shelly. "I cannot roll over. You are so lucky."

"But Shelly," said Pearl, "Not every animal does the same things. You have to find your own talent."
Shelly nodded, but looked sad. Pearl dove back into the mud.

Splash!
"I'll see you later, Pearl," said Shelly. She went on her way.

Next, Shelly saw Carla the Cow.
"Mooooooo!" said Carla. "Hello Shelly! Listen to how loud I can be!"
"MOOOOOO!"
"Wow Carla!" said Shelly. "You are very loud! What a great talent!"
"You can be loud, too," said Carla. "Just lift your head and shout."

Shelly lifted her little turtle head as high as it would go.
She took a big breath, and let it all out.
"SQUEAK!" All that came out was one little noise. Shelly put her head
back down. "I can never be loud like you, Carla," she said.
"I'm just not good at anything."

"Mooooo," said Carla. "Just keep trying.
Every animal is good at something."

"I guess," said Shelly.
She walked slowly away.

"Horses are fast, pigs can play in the dirt, and cows can moo," said Shelly to herself. "I wish I could be like them."
Just then, there was a loud noise. **BOOM!** Thunder clapped through the sky. Then raindrops started to fall.
"Oh no!" yelled Harold the Horse. "I can't run in the rain! I might slip!"

"The rain is washing away all of my mud!"
 shouted Pearl the Pig.
"You can't hear me moo over the sound of the storm,"
 sighed Carla the Cow.
 The animals all scurried around to try to find shelter.

But Shelly didn't need to scurry at all. Shelly pulled her legs into her shell. **"Pop! Pop! Pop! Pop!"** Then she lowered her head, and brought it inside, too.

It was nice and warm inside the shell. And best of all, it was dry! The rain could not get Shelly in here.

"Shelly!" called the other animals. "You are so lucky! You have a built-in shelter!" Shelly looked out at them. For the first time, they all wanted to be like her!

"You're right!" said Shelly.
"We're all special in our own way."

All day Shelly had wanted
to be good at something,
and the answer was right
on her back the whole time.
From that day on, she knew
that she was special too.

"Now I can play!"
Jeannie said with a shout.
"Now I can finally, FINALLY go out!"

"They're not in the closet,
 Where else could they hide?"
 Then she stopped, and turned,
 And smiled nice and wide.

Of all of the places,
Every cranny and nook,
The closet was one place
She never did look.
She opened the door,
And there were her shoes!
The most obvious place,
Without any clues.

standing on her head.

Jeannie looked in her bedroom,
And under the bed.
She looked under the dresser,

No sign of the shoes.
She sighed a big sigh.
Those two smelly shoes
Must be awfully shy!

Jeannie looked on the porch,
And in the back yard.
This looking and looking
Was getting quite hard!

She looked in the corner,
But no shoes at all.

She looked in the bathtub.
Then looked down the hall.

She looked at her dog,
Who gave her a wink.

She looked in the kitchen.
And looked in the sink.

29 years that God gave her on this earth, she lived life to the fullest, fulfilling her dreams and helping to make the world a better place.

After her death, two memorials were established by her friends, associates and family. A park bench was dedicated in her honor at the Eclipse Lagoon of the Rockford Park District in Illinois. A scholarship in Jeannie's name will be awarded annually by Marquette University to a student in the College of Communication.

This book is based on two stories that Jeannie wrote and entered into a children's story contest shortly before her death. Jeannie's Missing Shoes was originally titled Tom's Missing Shoes; however, the publisher and Jeannie's family decided to change the name and main character in her honor as a legacy of her love for her family and friends.

About the Illustrators

Angie Scordato is the proud mother of five sons. Amazingly, she still finds time to pursue her passion as a professional Artist. Angie is well known for her portraits, home/business murals, canvas work and as an illustrator of fine children's books including, Smemory (2013) and Namaste: A Little Yoga Folks Tale (2013). Blessed with God-given talent, Angie is a self-taught artist whose love of God and family shines through her work.

Jeff Gale has been drawing since the late 60's. He has a light-hearted view of the world. His drawings depict a gentle universe of humor, innocence, peace, love and friendship. In 2002 after 34 years, Jeff retired from teaching elementary and middle school art. He has illustrated a series of alphabet books and Universe of You (2012). He's still happily drawing away and enjoys taking long walks in the woods by his home. He lives with his wife, Peggy, in Loves Park, Illinois, near their daughter and her family. Jeff went to great lengths to include special mementos of Jeannie throughout the illustrations. He hopes you seek, find, and enjoy each and every one!

This book is dedicated to Jeannie's niece, Tess,
whom she adored and who turned one year old the day after Jeannie died,
and to her nephew, David, who was born four months later.

About the Author

† *February 15, 1983-November 8, 2012*

Jeannie Marie Hayes was born in Shreveport, Louisiana in 1983. She moved to South Bend, Indiana in the sixth grade and then attended Penn High School, where she played flute in the marching band and worked as a reporter in the school's TV station. She continued to pursue her interest in television at Marquette University, where she graduated in 2005 with a bachelor's degree in broadcast communication.

After college, Jeannie started working as a producer at WREX-TV in Rockford, Illinois. During the seven years she was there, she anchored the weekend and noon shows and hosted "13 Cares," a community outreach program at the station. In 2012, Jeannie also co-anchored the morning show on B103 Radio. She had thousands of followers.

Best known for her "infectious" smile, sense of humor, and non-confrontational demeanor, Jeannie made the most of her strong writing and communications skills. Inspired by Oprah, Jeannie had a passion for telling positive stories and helping local community organizations. She was patient and kind to people, reaching out to many through social media. She had a special love for animals as well, and literally would never hurt a fly.

Sadly and without warning, Jeannie was diagnosed with a very aggressive type of acute myeloid leukemia. She died on November 8th, 2012, just two days later. In the

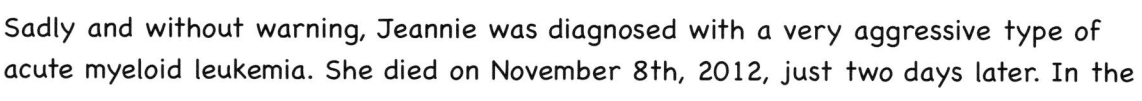

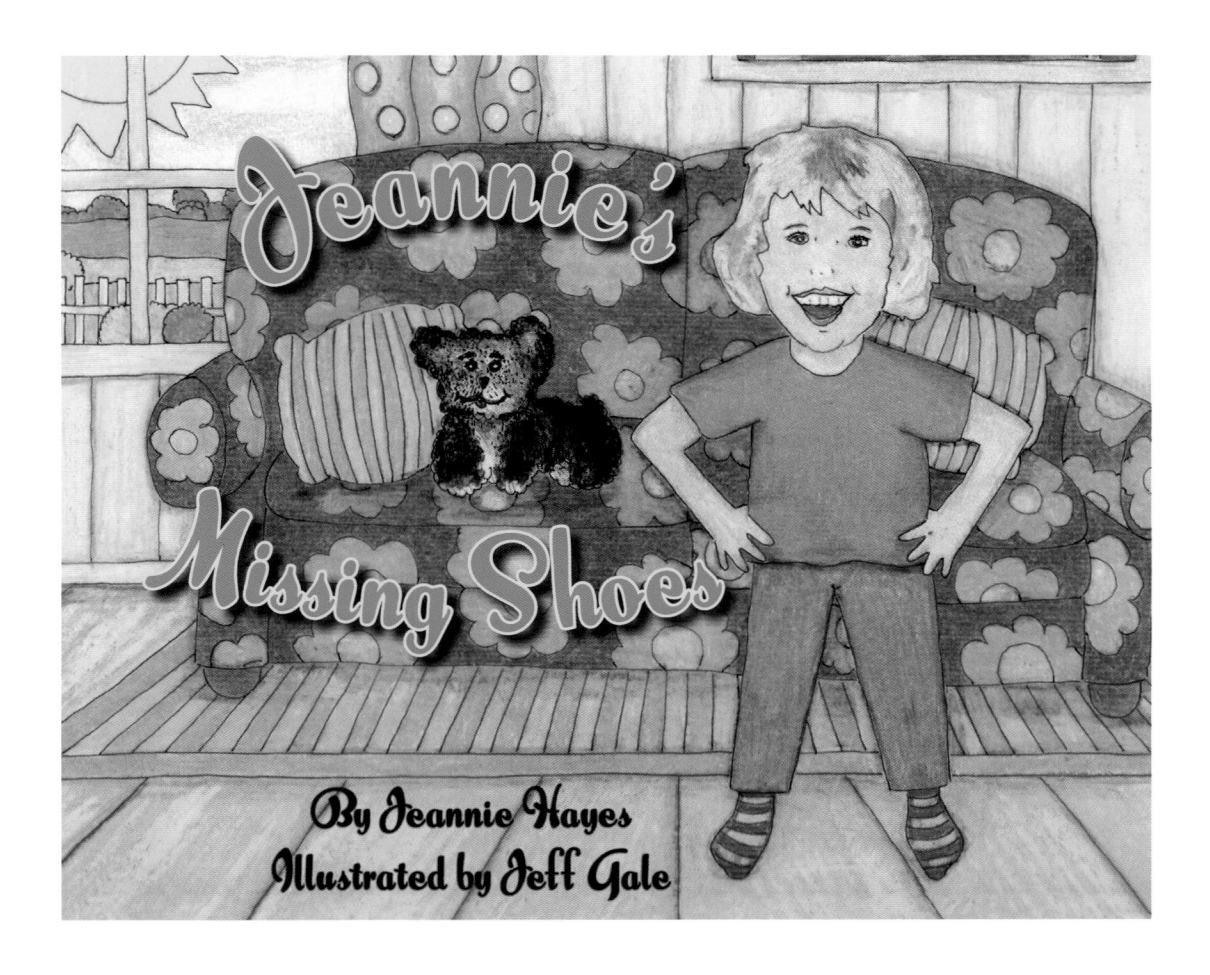

Jeannie's Missing Shoes

By Jeannie Hayes

Illustrated by Jeff Gale